SOMEDAY

T S ARTHUR

Copyright © 2024 T S Arthur
All rights reserved.

COVER DESIGN BY: Irish Ink Publishing

Copyright © **T S Arthur** 2024
Published by **T S Arthur**

The right of **T S Arthur** to be identified as the author of this work has been asserted by her under the Copyright Amendment (Moral Rights) Act 2000.

License Notes: This novel is licensed for your personal enjoyment only. This print may not be re-sold or given away to other people. If you would like to share this book with another person, please purchase an additional copy for each recipient. If you're reading this book and did not purchase it, or it was not purchased for your use only, then please purchase your own copy. Thank you for respecting the hard work of this author. This book is a work of fiction and any resemblance to persons, living or dead, or places, events or locales is purely coincidental. The characters are productions of the author's imagination and used fictitiously. This work is copyright. Apart from any use as permitted under the Copyright Act 1968, no part may be reproduced, copied, scanned, stored in a retrieval system, recorded or transmitted, in any form or by any means, without the prior written permission of the publisher.
All similarities to names, places, and events are purely coincidental.

AUTHOR'S NOTE

Hello!

So, for the first time ever, I felt it was necessary to drop a little note before you read this book. Please don't read this if you prefer not to see spoilers or trigger warnings.

There are some themes in Someday which might be upsetting, and so I wanted to make sure you were aware of that before you started reading. I respect that everyone's experiences are different, so please use the following information to make an informed choice which suits your needs.

Georgie, our main character, will grapple with a number of issues, which include:

- loss of a partner
- postnatal depression

If you have been impacted by these themes, there are some useful websites with resources here:

https://www.cruse.org.uk/
https://pandasfoundation.org.uk/

AUTHOR'S NOTE

https://www.mind.org.uk/

Please note, as I am based in the UK, these are charities and organisations from the UK, but there will be similar places in your home country. Always seek support if you need it.

If you've ever suffered a loss which turns your world so completely on its head that happiness seems impossible, this one is for you.

It will get better, I promise.

PROLOGUE

"Come along now, children. Let's get into a circle. Quickly!"

The friendly-looking teacher clapped her hands and chivvied the late-comers into the spaces. Her mousy hair was wispy and showed the telltale signs of having done yet another break duty in the wind. Her brown eyes were dull behind her hand as she rubbed her forehead, trying to chase away a headache. It had been one of those weeks—one of those months, in fact—and she was more than ready for the home time bell.

If truth be told, the classroom wasn't really suitable for a circle of thirty children, but there was no space for her to do it elsewhere. Cuts were being made all over the school. She'd had no time to replan her lessons after the heating had packed up and left the older children using the hall as a classroom. All she wanted was an easy Friday afternoon. That was why she was making the best of the situation and improvising for a lesson that wouldn't require her to tote large bags of marking home for the weekend.

"Mrs Barber! Billy pushed me out of the circle." A small

child with blonde curls and amber eyes pouted up at her, pulling on her sleeve to get her attention.

"Billy, dear, move along and let poor Georgie back in, please." She was at the end of her tether with these two children. They seized every opportunity to antagonise each other, and she had had quite enough of their bickering for one day.

"But, Miiissss," whined the little girl at her side. "I don't want to sit by him anymore. He's a meanie."

"Oh, for goodness sake! Go and sit by Micheal instead then, but just find a seat and do it quickly," she said as she turned her back to the class and took a long drink from her 'best teacher' mug. Imagining it contained more than just cold coffee, she closed her eyes for a moment and went to her happy place.

"Right then, children. This afternoon, we're going to talk about what you'd like to be when you're older. Would anyone like to start us off?"

She glanced around at the small children in front of her. Some were listening, others were gazing into space—the usual suspects, of course. Some were obviously deep in thought, but then it was a big question for a six-year-old.

"I do, Miss," came a quiet voice she'd rather had kept quiet. Billy McIntyre was 'that' child. The one who everyone in school had known the name of since the end of his first week. A year later, he still hadn't changed, and she doubted he ever would. Forcing a smile, Mrs Barber nodded her head in his direction.

"Well, I wanna be a race car driver so I can have cars what goes vroom and fast like on them races me dad watches." He beamed proudly, the gappy smile of a child who was on top of the world. She fought to hide her surprise. It was actually a sensible answer from him for once.

"A lovely idea, Billy. Anyone else?" She was already beginning to wonder if she might regret this plan.

The children passed the tatty lion teddy around the circle. Some played with its ears as they talked, others threw it to their friends with a little too much gusto, but on the whole, they stayed orderly. Finally, after what felt like a monotonous procession of dull and predictable answers, the whiny girl from earlier sat playing with the once fluffy mane of the toy.

"Well, Georgie, we're waiting." She nudged the child gently to speak.

Georgie looked up with wide eyes and a scared smile. Georgie Carpenter was one of her favourite students, despite her propensity to moan about every little thing. She was a classic teacher's pet, but not in an annoying way. Mrs Barber returned her smile, and the girl took a deep breath and began to speak.

"I want to be a mummy and have lots of babies and look after 'em real good," she said. Colour filled her little round cheeks as the room fell silent. At least it was until…

"A mummy isn't a real job, stupid!" Billy shouted.

His usual irritating behaviour had returned, and the room erupted in laughter. Georgie hid her face in the lion she was still holding, and Mrs Barber fought to regain control of the now excitable class of children. Admitting defeat, she breathed a sigh of relief when the bell rang for home time, and she was free of the hassle until Monday morning.

As she oversaw returning the children to their parents, she pondered on the little girl's answer. It was one she hadn't heard before, and after years of doing this activity with countless children, it filled her heart with a little dose of joy. Children like Georgie Carpenter were the reason she did this job.

ONE

"So what do we do now then? You just pee on it and it tells us whether you're cooking a bun or not?" said Billy, his casual manner failing miserably to convince Georgie that he wasn't bothered in the slightest that she might be pregnant. As if to prove a point, he ran his hand through his scruffy black hair.

"Yes, you daft prat. I pee on the stick and the pregnancy fairy pops up and tells us whether there's a bun in there or not." She rolled her eyes as she spoke, laughing internally at his slack-jawed expression. Georgie gave him a quick peck on the cheek before closing the bathroom door in his face.

"That's gross," he said from behind the door.

"If you think that's bad, you don't want to know what else is going to happen over the next nine months if this is positive." She heard a gagging noise and nearly peed all over her hand instead of the stick as a chuckle ripped out of her. "I mean it! There's mucus plugs and breaking waters and all sorts of other nasties. Don't you remember anything from biology?" she asked, setting the blue and white plastic stick on the sink and washing her hands.

Georgie opened the door, causing Billy to fall backwards.

He must have been leaning against it. His face was such a contrast of emotions. Fear, excitement, shock, happiness—each battled with the others to create a peculiar expression.

"How long do we wait?" Billy shuffled up so there was space for her to sit beside him in the door frame.

"Not long. What if it's, you know…" Worry ate away at her. She'd only just finished university and still didn't have a steady job. They had no family, at least none they spoke to. How would they cope with a baby?

"It will be an adventure." His beaming face said it all; he couldn't have been happier. The smile fell when he caught sight of her frown. "Do you… is this not…"

"I don't know, Billy. Are we really ready for this? We can hardly keep ourselves alive sometimes. How can we be responsible for a tiny human? Maybe we should get a dog first, something to practise on, you know?" Georgie chewed at her lip, her nails clacking against the tiled floor.

"Stop. Look at me." He took her hands in his and waited for her to make eye contact. When she did, he leaned forward and placed a kiss on her forehead before moving to each cheek, and finally her lips. "Whatever happens, we're in this together, right? Besides, you couldn't stand me at school and now you can't live without me. We can do anything—no, everything—we want to do. I love you, Georgie."

He kissed her again, his tongue teasing her chapped lips open. A fervour took over him. Deepening the kiss, he put a hand at the base of her neck and pulled her closer. When they broke away, her knitted brows had unravelled, and Georgie felt the tightness in her face loosen.

Without a word, she stood and retrieved the test. She turned it over, hiding the result until they were sitting next to each other. Billy stretched an arm around her, reaching to join his hands and rest them on her stomach. He kissed the back of her neck before resting his chin on her shoulder.

"Whatever happens?" she questioned.

"Whatever happens," he repeated.

It was their mantra, something they'd said to each other since they'd first got together as teenagers. No one had expected it, not given how they'd bickered and clashed as children. But when Georgie had watched Billy dive headfirst into a river to save a dog on a school trip, something had changed. He wasn't just Billy McIntyre, class clown and giant pain in the arse. He became Billy, the boy who rescued furry friends.

Soon after that, she had stepped up to him after school and asked him to join her for a Big Mac. He'd never let her forget the stuttering way she'd asked. Or the fact her friends had shouted all sorts of obscenities when they'd walked past and caught them sharing their first kiss. It had been a peck on the cheek, an awkward gesture she'd prompted, but of course, they'd seen them.

"So, what does it say?" he prompted.

She jumped, lost in thoughts of simpler times, when all they'd had to worry about were jealous friends and when a history essay was due. Inhaling deeply, she held her breath as she turned the test over. A little window had typed letters. They danced before her eyes and she struggled to make sense of it.

"Well? I can't see it. Give it here." He snatched the plastic from her hand, all earlier squeamishness about the fact she had peed on it gone. "Oh my God! It's positive. Look, it says it here—pregnant! Georgie, you're going to be a mummy, just like you always wanted."

Billy leaped up, knocking her head into the doorframe. She barely registered the blow, a hand reaching up on instinct to rub the tender spot.

"Pregnant..." she whispered, the news not seeming real. "Are you sure?"

"Absolutely. It says it right here. These things are pretty nifty. You don't even have to figure out how many lines it is.

Baby, we're having a baby! Haha, that's... wow! A baby!" Billy continued to dance around, waving the stick in the air with a grin wider than any she'd seen on his face before. Even his joy at pranking people couldn't draw a smile this big.

"Yeah, a baby. I'm going to be a mummy," she said, trying to absorb his excitement and channel it into her response. Her lips forced themselves into a semblance of happiness, but she was certain it would look more like a grimace. Georgie looked down at her stomach and gulped.

Billy finally noticed her disconnect. "Aren't you... happy?" His brows furrowed and he dropped to his knees, cupping her face. "I thought this was what you'd always wanted. Way back when we were six, and all through school, you talked about being a mother. I thought you'd be... well, happier than this."

Georgie sighed. "I am, it's just a lot to wrap my head around. I've got no real job, you're always away with work, and there's a living thing growing inside me. I did always want to be a mum. I still do. I guess I just thought we'd have a bit more time being just the two of us."

"Baby, if everyone waited until the perfect time to have kids, no one would ever have them. They come when they're wanted, not when they're convenient. At least, that's what Gran always said."

"I know, and I'm happy, I swear. It's just a shock."

Billy stroked Georgie's cheek, tucking her long blonde fringe behind her ear. "I hear you. But this is a gift. It's special. You're going to make the best mummy out there, just you wait and see."

Georgie rested her forehead against his, her long hair falling forward to cover her face for a moment. She let a solitary tear fall. It was what she'd wanted, he was right, but it was also too soon in her life plan. Babies were meant to come when they had steady jobs, and a stable home to welcome the child into. They lived in a building site of a half-renovated shack with barely enough cash for food.

Worries washed over her but she buried them beneath the waves of panic that kept hitting the shores of her mind. It would be all right, wouldn't it? People like them had babies all the time and it always worked out okay in the end. Usually. Didn't it?

TWO

THE PALE PINK WALLS OF THE WAITING ROOM WERE MORE GAUDY than calming, and the chairs were definitely not as comfortable as they looked. Georgie's appointment was supposed to have been half an hour ago, but her name still hadn't been called. Billy was bouncing around in his chair, checking the time on his phone every couple of minutes.

She wished she could have the excitement he did. Although Georgie was happy about the fact she was pregnant, she couldn't pretend she was as overjoyed as Billy. But maybe seeing the baby on the screen at her first scan today would help her connect with the tiny human in her stomach. The tiny human who had made her spend two hours a day with her head in a toilet bowl and sleep the rest of it.

"Georgie Carpenter," a woman called from the end of the corridor.

Billy shot up. "Here! She's here." He turned to her and said, "Come on, Georgie. It's our turn."

Georgie spotted a few other mums-to-be sniggering, others watched with a soppy look in their eyes. No doubt they wished their partners had the same excitement. Billy was the only man in the waiting room acting like a kid about to hit the motherlode under the Christmas tree. She should have been amused—this was typical Billy—but instead, it lit a spark of annoyance. It burned slowly, fanned by the rampant hormones that controlled her.

"I'm coming," Georgie grumbled at him. "And can you calm down? You're embarrassing." His face twisted in pain, and she regretted her words in an instant. "Sorry. Hormones." It was her excuse for everything. How he put up with it, she had no idea.

"Hi, Georgie. I'm Jane and I'll be doing your ultrasound today. If you want to hop up on the bed, your companion can sit there, and we'll get started." She waited for the paper to stop crinkling and for Georgie to roll up her top before she spoke again. "The gel will be a bit cold, sorry."

Billy shuffled the chair closer and leaned on the edge of the bed, his hand reaching for Georgie's. His palm was sweaty and his arm was full of restless energy. Jane spotted it and smiled.

"I'm guessing this is your first?"

"How could you tell?" Georgie asked, sarcasm lacing her voice.

Jane tilted her head towards Billy. "We don't get many dads this excited. Especially when it's not their first like you guys. They know what's coming." She laughed and pointed to the screen suspended above the bed. "Baby will pop up on there. I'll do some measurements and then we can get a picture if you like. Shall we get started?"

Georgie nodded and glanced at Billy. His chestnut eyes shone with delight, which was adorable. She couldn't deny that now she was about to see their baby, there was a spark of excitement that suddenly appeared in her chest.

"We're about to see our baby," she said. The realisation that the last few weeks had all been a blur hit her, a solid wall of emotions crashing into her as she waited for the screen to load. Tears escaped, but Billy wiped them away with his thumb.

"Yeah, we are." He leaned his forehead against hers and then nudged her to look at the screen.

Black and grey blobs danced before their eyes, though she'd hazard a guess neither of them knew what they were. The room was silent except for the clicking of the sonographer and Georgie's rapid breathing. Billy's foot tapped out a steady rhythm on the tiled floor, which made Georgie tut. It was typical Billy, though. He never could sit still, even as a kid.

"And there we are! Hello, little one," said Jane. She pointed to the screen nearest to her as she spoke. "There's baby's head, and that's their hands, their body, and their legs. Measurements are all looking good. Did you want a picture?"

"Yes, please." They spoke simultaneously, a loud cry from Billy making Jane laugh. Georgie felt the infectious enthusiasm and allowed herself to get swept up in his happiness.

"Not a problem. Let's get a good shot for you," Jane said with a smile. She focused on the apparatus again before declaring herself done. She passed Georgie a piece of tissue to remove the excess gel and turned to her computer. After a few seconds of typing, she said, "Here's your picture. If you head back to the waiting room, they'll call you again as soon as they can."

"Aren't we finished?" Billy asked. They'd already been there an hour and Georgie assumed he must be getting bored. Or hungry. He was always one of the two.

"Sadly not. There are a few more people to see. It's always worse at the first scan." She flashed them a friendly look and waited for them to leave.

"Thank you," Georgie said, pulling Billy towards the door. "Don't be rude. It's not her fault they're running late."

"No, I know that."

They returned to their original seats, Georgie sighing as she sat. It would be even more uncomfortable as the baby caused her stomach to grow. She looked to her left and spotted Billy had already got the scan photo out on his lap. He traced its outline with his finger before he caught her watching him.

His phone rang, piercing the touching moment. Passing her the piece of paper, he gave her an apologetic smile and headed for the corridor. Phones weren't supposed to be used in this area, but everyone else had theirs out. Most weren't on calls, though.

With nothing to do and no one to talk to, Georgie glanced at the image of their baby. It would have been smaller than this inside her, the size of a plum according to an app Billy had downloaded. Yet this picture had it looking much larger. She could see the start of a little face, see the tiny fingers hovering near the mouth.

Would it be a thumb sucker? Would it have her practical mind or Billy's excitable one? Who would it look like? Would it be a boy or a girl?

Questions swirled in her mind, kindling the spark of excitement that had appeared from nowhere earlier. Finally, she felt happy about their situation. They were having a baby. They would be parents.

Memories of those cruel jokes at school for her desires didn't matter now. They were useless and she discarded them, letting her mind fill with happier images.

She and Billy cradling a small bundle that grew into a toddler taking its first steps. Billy chasing it in the park as it learned how to ride a bike with no stabilisers. The image shifted and it was a little girl begging her daddy for a piggyback, then a little boy wanting a race car for his birthday. Flashes of their home came next, rooms filled with toys and washing drying, and happy laughter. There was more than just the babe she now carried; the house was filled with children. Their children.

Their future had shifted. Georgie might have planned for more adventures just the two of them, or even for a higher amount on their savings account, but it didn't matter. All that did was the baby inside her and Billy. With them, she could have everything she had ever wanted.

Finally, she felt that first glow of pregnancy she'd read about. Life had so much to give her and as she rubbed her stomach and gazed at the plum-sized baby on the sonogram, An overwhelming sensation of love bubbled within her, overflowing when Billy returned and wrapped his arms around her, resting his hands above their unborn child.

THREE

Life had settled into a steady pattern. When Billy woke, he brought Georgie a cup of tea and two slices of toast with just the tiniest scraping of butter and marmalade. It was all she could stomach before noon, and even then it was a struggle for her to keep it down. The further through the pregnancy she went, the easier it became, though.

Billy would peck her on the cheek, kiss the growing bump, and then work on the house if he could. It was their top priority now the baby was coming. They couldn't bring a child home to bare floorboards and half-plastered walls.

Most of the time, though, Billy would leave for the day, or sometimes days. His work as a junior mechanic in a racing team kept him busy and often meant he had to travel to far-flung locations. At Georgie's request, he'd asked for a change of duties, but his employer was dragging their heels. All she wanted was for him to be safe in the UK base, close to home in case she needed him.

She'd known all along Billy would be a free spirit. At school, he'd declared his love of fast cars aged just five and now he'd finally got an opportunity to realise his dream. Billy had been offered a chance to drive a Formula Three car. It was a one-off, a reward for his initiative and constant eagerness to impress, but he was almost as excited for this as he was for their baby.

"I'll be back by the weekend. Are you sure you're going to be okay?" He hovered around the bed, smoothing the sheets and tucking her hair behind her ears.

"I'll be fine. The baby isn't going to come for weeks yet, and I'm getting stronger now I can keep my breakfast down. I will miss having breakfast in bed. though," Georgie teased. It was the truth—this luxury was easy to get used to.

Billy laughed. "However will you survive, your ladyship?" He gave a low bow and held his hand out for hers. She placed it in his, and like the period dramas she made him watch, he brushed his lips against her knuckles.

"With great difficulty, dear sir. But seriously, Billy, you better go. Being late for your flight isn't going to be the best move. Trust me, we'll be fine. Call me when you're there, promise?" She squeezed his hand, reluctant to let him leave. As much as she told him she'd cope without him, if she was honest, she was petrified.

"Okay, I'm going. Don't forget to eat, and drink, and don't do anything stupid. No lifting boxes or spending a fortune on nursery decorations." He winked and she laughed, knowing full well it was him who was obsessed with spending money on a child that hadn't even arrived yet. Every day, she came home to another package of something he'd read about online and decided the baby couldn't live without.

"Stay safe, love. I miss you already." Georgie pulled his hand to her face and leaned into his cupped palm. She should have got up and seen him to the door, but watching him leave the bedroom would be hard enough. Swallowing the tears, she put on a brave front. "Now go. I'll see you soon."

Billy slipped his free hand behind her head and pulled her lips up to meet his. She sighed as he kissed her, a passionate goodbye that woke her dull senses and made her stomach flip.

"I love you," she said.

"I love you two," he replied, smiling at their little inside joke.

"We love you," Georgie corrected, rolling her eyes at his silly routine.

With a final kiss for both her and the bump, Billy turned and left. A shiver ran down Georgie's spine when she heard the door shut behind him. It never got easier letting him go.

Although Georgie had always supported Billy's career, she had grown more aware over recent years of just how dangerous motor racing could be. Whilst safety innovations were always forthcoming and Billy wasn't in the driving seat yet, accidents could still happen. This was the first time he'd had to travel since she'd found out she was pregnant, but she had a feeling it might happen more.

Only a handful of the mechanics had been given this chance, and only those who held the right licences. Billy took his test as soon as he could, having worked his way through the karting circuits. It had cost his parents a fortune and she knew it caused Billy great distress that neither of them had survived to see his dreams coming true.

She secretly hoped their child wouldn't be as interested in racing as Billy was. Watching them religiously each week was one thing, as was travelling to circuits to see them live. But having to watch her baby hurtle around at hundreds of miles an hour? No, thank you.

The force of the feeling made Georgie pause. Up until then, the baby had been mostly an abstract thing. She'd felt a connection from looking at the scan photo, which had become her lock screen on her phone, but it was fleeting. Everything she'd read online hinted that she would have this instant bond, but she was struggling.

Pregnancy was harder than she'd expected. The aches and

sickness were more manageable, but the exhaustion was making life difficult. She was able to work flexibly which was a godsend, but even her employer had noticed something was off. Only she and Billy knew, and a few of his colleagues. She'd decided to wait until after the scan to share the news, but she kept putting it off.

The phone buzzed on the bedside table, disturbing her from her thoughts. She chugged the now-cold tea and waited for it to stop vibrating before she picked it up. Munching on a slice of toast, Georgie listened to the voicemail message.

"Georgie, we need you in the office for a chat. Can you make it in today?"

The caller left no name or number but they didn't need to. Bruce only called when it was serious. Either she'd been more absent than she'd anticipated, or a client had made a complaint. She needed this job; perhaps it was time to come clean about the pregnancy.

Georgie hopped out of bed and headed straight for the bathroom. Brushing her teeth and sucking on a peppermint to help the nausea, she rummaged in her wardrobe. Whilst her bump wasn't immediately noticeable in most outfits, figure-hugging ones made it quite obvious she was pregnant. Opting for the most fitted dress she owned, Georgie checked her reflection, grabbed her work things from her home office, and set off.

Her physical office was a short walk from their house, and in the warmth of the morning, she quickly worked up a sweat. Hopefully, she'd meet with Bruce and he'd back off once he knew about the baby. If he didn't... She wouldn't think about that, not yet.

Georgie pulled her hair into a loose bun, relishing the brief relief it brought her. She stood outside the building for a moment, looking up at the glass front. Recruitment had never been her first choice but she'd fallen into it and it paid the bills. Feigning a confidence she didn't possess, Georgie plastered on a smile and strolled through the door and straight up to Bruce's office. Gazes followed her but she ignored them.

"Bruce, you wanted to see me?" she said, standing in his doorway.

He spun on his chair, mouth gaping as he looked at her. "Georgie. Yes. Hi. Come in," he said, fumbling around to get her a chair and a glass of water. She sipped at it, resisting the urge to gulp it down. "We haven't seen you in the office for a while and we wanted to check in."

"That's kind of you. I was under the impression that as long as the work was done, I didn't have to come into the office." Georgie played it coy but knew full well there was no contractual stipulation for in-person attendance.

"Very true, but HR thought we ought to touch base. It's been a few months…" He trailed off, rubbing the back of his neck before he continued, "Is everything okay with you and Billy?"

Georgie fought the urge to laugh. Bruce would never come out and ask her if she was pregnant, he was too conscious of doing things by the book, not asking the wrong things. But she knew what he was hinting at. "It's better than okay. We're expecting."

Bruce's face changed in an instant. The blundering concern was replaced with joy. Why was it that everyone was happy when you told them there was a baby? It didn't matter if they knew you or not, they all claimed a slice of happiness from the news.

"Why, that's wonderful. We'll need to let HR know, but I assume that's why you've been working from home more. And the reason for the missed deadlines."

"Yes, I've been finding some symptoms a little tricky. In fact, I need to—"

"Not at all. Go, I'll clear it all. And congratulations. If you need anything, you know where I am."

Georgie nodded with a smile. "Thank you, Bruce. It means a lot to know you're so understanding." She stood and walked to the door, making a show of stopping off at the bathroom on the way out.

No doubt her inbox would be full of messages as soon as the jungle drums were in motion. She wasn't that bothered. At least it would keep Bruce off her back. Maybe there were some perks to this pregnancy malarkey after all. Mind racing, she began to wonder whether now might be the right time to look at a career change. With Bruce relaxing expectations she could start training to achieve her dreams.

"Stick with me, little one. We'll do grand, you and me, just you wait," she said once she was home. Georgie pulled out the laptop, opened a search engine, and began to plan her future.

FOUR

EACH MONDAY STARTED WITH A DISCUSSION ABOUT WHICH FRUIT the baby was this week. Billy had started it, but Georgie had downloaded an app now too. She enjoyed the insights it gave her into what the baby was doing and how it was developing. Bonding with an abstract idea of what was, in her mind, an alien growing inside her had been difficult. But knowing it was now making fists and sucking its thumb helped Georgie realise it was real.

It had become a race to see who could announce the fruit or vegetable when the new one popped up on the app. They were eating breakfast together in the kitchen when the notifications pinged simultaneously.

"Bell pepper!" Georgie shouted, just pipping Billy to it.

She hopped off her chair without another word and rummaged in the fridge, appearing a few moments later with a red pepper. Holding it in front of her small but rapidly growing bump, she laughed when Billy pulled out his phone and snapped a picture. Everything felt perfect. Happiness washed over her, submerging her and buoying her mood.

"I've been thinking—" Billy started, but Georgie interrupted him.

"Always a dangerous way to start a day. Especially for you."

"Hush, you. As I said, I've been thinking…we're almost half way along. Do you think we should start looking at names?"

A blade of worry sliced through Georgie's flawless moment. To name it before it came was contributing to that abstract thought pattern. It fed her anxiety and left her chewing on the inside of her cheek.

"Isn't it too soon?"

"No, I don't think so. There have been babies born as early as twenty-one weeks that have survived. It wouldn't hurt to have some ideas at least. We don't have to decide today."

Georgie thought about his idea, munching on her toast in silence. Eventually, she looked up. Billy had been watching her, a grin on his face.

"You're beautiful, did you know that?" he said, his eyes soft and filled with adoration.

"Pfft, give over." She stuck her tongue out at him. "I suppose it wouldn't be a bad thing to have a few names ready. At least then if we can't decide. we've got enough time to find others." A nudge of happiness prompted her to half-raise her lips in a smile. "What did you have in mind?"

Billy leapt forward, opening a note on his phone. He dragged the chair noisily round so it was right beside her and showed Georgie a list of names.

"Really? How long have you had this?" she asked with a laugh.

"Er, I'm not sure you want to know." Billy scratched his head and looked at the floor. When she didn't speak, he filled the silence. "A week before the scan… I know, I know!" he added when she glared at him. "I'm excited, all right? Bite me." Billy poked his tongue out at her but didn't move fast enough to avoid a nip on his shoulder.

"What?" she replied to his incredulous gaze. "You told me

to. Let's look at this list, then." Georgie flicked through, giggling at some, nodding at others. He'd got a good mix of boys and girls, some with racing connections, and others she had never heard him mention. At the top of each list were three in bold. "Are these your favourites?" she asked.

"Yeah. So, for a boy, I like Sebastian, Michael, and Murray. And for a girl, I like Hannah, Jamie, and Ruby."

"Hmm. Hannah for your mum, right?" Billy gave a sad bob of the head. "I love that idea. It's a great way to include her even though…"

"She's not here. I know. That's the worst part of all this. I'm so excited and I want to tell everyone, but the one person I want to share it with more than anyone else is Mum. But she's not here. It's hard, you know?" He sighed and looked up. It was his usual trick when he was trying to stop himself from crying.

Georgie reached out and pulled his head to rest on her chest. "She'd be so proud of you. Hannah for a girl. I'm not sure on a boy's name yet, though. Those ones you've picked aren't doing it for me."

When she said 'Hannah', the gentle swirling and fluttering sensations she'd been feeling for the last few days got stronger.

"Billy! I think… I think it's moving. I think I can feel it."

He dropped to his knees before her and placed his hands on her stomach. "Oh my God! Do it again, baby. Show Daddy, please," he crooned to her belly button.

"It was when you said Hannah. Say it again. Talk through your names." Georgie's excitement built. This was the most real the baby had felt since the scan. The thrill of knowing it was alive and well within the safety of her womb sent a buzz of elation through her, radiating from her bump.

"What d'you say, kid? Hannah? Or are you a Sebastian?"

"It did it again!" she squealed. "I felt it. I felt it move!"

Billy looked up at her with his big brown eyes. She didn't

need him to say it; she knew how very much in love with her he was. How much he loved the unborn babe. In that moment, it was like they were one, both joined in their happiness.

"Can I?" he asked, his hand hovering over her bump.

"Of course you can, you daft sod. It's your baby."

"Our baby," he said, placing his hand on her stomach. Georgie smiled as she guided his palm so it was above where she felt the infant was. She couldn't say for certain how she knew it was there, but she just knew.

"Can you feel it?" she asked, her eyebrows pulling together. Billy sat still, patiently waiting to feel the being moving inside her. He shook his head and she sighed. "I'm sorry, love. I thought you might be able to feel it too."

"It's okay. As soon as his legs get stronger, we'll be feeling him in no time."

"Him? What makes you think that?" Georgie took his hand in hers and helped him from his crouched position.

"Just a hunch."

"Hmm." She lifted an eyebrow at him in silent question, but he resumed eating, not even grumbling about his now soggy cereal.

A roguish grin lit up his face. He'd be a fantastic dad, regardless of whether the baby was a boy or a girl, or whatever it decided to be when it grew up. The love he already had for this child overwhelmed Georgie. How could anyone love something—no, someone— they'd never met so much?

It had taken until today for her to begin to comprehend that she had a baby living inside her. Now she'd felt it, though, something had changed within her. It was real. It was happening. The scan had helped bring a sliver of light, but this had ripped the curtains wide open, letting in the bright light of day. The shade she'd lived under was removed.

Now she'd accepted the fact this was happening, the fact

she was nearly halfway through this pregnancy, Georgie kicked herself for having wasted so much time pretending it wasn't real. How could she have squandered so many weeks of unbridled happiness? She should have been submerging herself in the earliest moments of motherhood, taking photos, reading books, filling her brain with everything she could learn about babies.

It was as if her thinking had shifted in an instant. Georgie knew what to do with the opportunity Bruce had given her. It would benefit her and the baby, and them as a family longer term. She would retrain as a midwife.

The combination of Billy's excitement, feeling her child for the first time, and deciding on a new path for her future left Georgie giddy. She wouldn't tell Billy just yet, but she decided she would spend some time today looking into courses. It would be her secret, a surprise for him once she'd found out all she needed to know.

FIVE

FINDING THE COURSE SHE WANTED TO DO HAD BEEN EASY. Joining it, however, proved more problematic. Georgie lacked certain subjects to get her onto a university course, and in all honesty, she wasn't sure she could cope with full-time study and a newborn. After a long chat with Billy, she decided to do an Access course which she could use once the baby was a little older. It would give her all the information she was craving but without being as intense.

She'd thought of nothing else in recent weeks, so it was a surprise when Billy's voice cut through her daydream whilst cooking that evening.

"Don't forget we've got the scan tomorrow. Am I picking you up or are you going to meet me there?"

"Scan? No, that's not this week, is it?" Georgie opened her calendar app on her phone and flicked through the days. How had she forgotten? She'd been looking forward to this one. "Damn."

"Don't get upset. You've been so busy with work and your course—"

"But I shouldn't be forgetting these things." She dropped her head into her hands and covered her face with the knotted mess that had replaced her curly blonde hair in recent weeks. Pregnancy hadn't given her the sleek locks she'd been told about.

Billy rose and pulled her into a hug, squeezing her shoulders but taking care not to put pressure on her bump. The baby kicked when he was near and he laughed at the tiny grimace on her face. Georgie wasn't used to the stronger motions yet.

"Baby brain. Embrace it, use it as an excuse. It's a real thing. Something to do with brain cells and blood flow or whatever," Billy said, grinning at the puzzled look she gave him. "I've got to dash, but I'll see you later. Love you two." He kissed her before dropping to his knees to brush his lips against her stomach.

THE WAITING ROOM WAS FULL OF MORE WOMEN, ALL IN different stages of pregnancy. Some looked ready to deliver there and then, others still with flat stomachs. Georgie wriggled on the chair, trying to get comfy. It was harder this time and her hips ached however she sat. Billy snorted, familiar with her routine. He'd described her last week as a dog padding its bedding—he wasn't far wrong, even if she'd given him a smack around the back of his head.

"Georgie Carpenter." It was a new face who had called her but she shot up, eager to see her baby once more. The contrast from last time didn't go unnoticed by Billy who trailed behind.

"Hello, Georgie. I'm Alison. If you can get on the bed, we'll get started."

She didn't need telling twice. As quickly as her stiff joints and large stomach would allow her, Georgie clambered onto the bed. Remembering the way she'd had to shuffle closer to the sonographer last time, she made sure to position herself just right.

"Oh, you're a good one," said Alison with a wink before she explained the things she'd be looking for in the scan. As it was their twenty-week one it was more in-depth. "There's one other thing... did you want to know the sex of the baby?"

"Yes," answered Georgie.

At the same time, Billy said, "No."

"What do you mean, no? Why wouldn't you want to know?" Georgie asked, her voice rising in pitch.

"Why would you? Don't you want the excitement until the very end?" Billy replied. He rubbed a hand over his brow. "Do you really want to know?"

Georgie sighed. "I do, but—"

They both turned to Alison, who had remained silent in their exchange. Georgie was certain she must have seen this sort of thing many times before judging from the knowing smile on Alison's face.

"Then you can." He directed his question to Alison. "Can you do that? Tell her but not me? I'll step out of the room or something."

"Yes, you wouldn't be the first. We aren't always accurate, so you do have to bear that in mind."

"We understand," Georgie replied, tilting her head so she faced Billy. "Are you sure you don't mind? What if I slip up and spoil the surprise?"

"You won't. I trust you," he said with a kiss and a gentle stroke of her forehead.

Georgie gave Alison a nod and focused on the screen. When the grey blobs appeared this time they were more easily recognisable as body parts. Billy squeezed her hand as they watched the baby kicking and sucking its thumb.

After what felt like forever, Alison declared all was well. "Dad, if you don't want to know, it might be best to step out now."

Billy's lips pressed against Georgie's forehead and she considered for a moment if she should go ahead with her plan. Could she keep something so important a secret for so long?

"Are you ready?" Alison asked.

Georgie bit her lip and closed her eyes for a moment before bobbing her head. "Yes, I want to know."

Her heart began to race as the image before her shifted again. She wiped her sweaty palms on the tissue at either side of her and waited for Alison to tell her what she wanted to hear. She didn't care whether the baby was a boy or a girl, she just wanted to know so she could plan, be prepared. It would make it harder with Billy not knowing, but she'd find a way.

"It's a boy."

The three simple words brought tears to her eyes. Georgie thought her heart would explode. With each new image, kick, or fact she learned about this baby, her love for it—him— grew. He kicked within her, his tiny feet tapping out a rhythm she had grown familiar with.

"Thank you," she whispered, taking the tissue offered to wipe the gel from her stomach.

Georgie took a moment to gather herself before she left the room, needing to control her emotions. It was going to be a hard run to the end of the pregnancy, but it was worth it. Already her head was full of images—Billy and their boy riding bikes, making their first go-kart. Their lives would be so much richer thanks to his arrival.

A boy.

She couldn't wait.

SIX

"Do you really need all this stuff?" Billy shouted from inside the boot of their car.

"Yes. Let me help." Georgie pushed her way past his outstretched arm. He looked at her like she was weak, vulnerable. "For God's sake, Billy. I'm pregnant, not dying. Let me help." Yet still he would not budge. "Look, what if I just tell you what bag to put where?"

Billy nodded reluctantly and stepped to the side, scratching at the back of his neck. He'd grown his hair out in recent weeks and the longer, chin-length style suited him. Georgie moved forward and directed him with an imperious tone. She'd been worse in recent weeks, possessed by a frenetic energy to have everything perfect. The nursery, the hospital bag, planning their route—everything had been fine-tuned to her liking. Not that she was satisfied; she redid it all every week.

"See?" Georgie raised an eyebrow in challenge.

"Yes, I see. I bow to your wisdom," Billy said, giving her a quick peck as he closed the boot. "Ready?"

"Ready. I can't wait for this weekend."

They climbed into the car, mounted Billy's phone as a sat

nav, and set off on their three-hour drive. The weekend had been planned for weeks, a final chance to indulge themselves before the baby arrived. Billy had wanted to spoil Georgie, so had organised the majority of it as a surprise. When he'd given her the details of the hotel and told her to choose whatever therapies she wanted, Georgie had squealed with delight.

Their hotel was nestled on the edge of a lake, surrounded by hills that overlooked like guardians of the water. Even without the mum-to-be massages and gourmet meals, the views alone would relieve her stresses. She was looking forward to spending hours on their balcony with a book, even if she would need a raincoat or a blanket against the British weather.

More than anything, Georgie wanted to spend time alone with Billy. His job had changed, taking him away more often. But it was the fact he now spent more time behind the wheel rather than in the garage. His promise at the incentive weekend a few months back had been shared with the right people.

When an opening arose as a reserve driver for a minor Formula Three team, Georgie had feigned pride and encouraged him to go for it. Inside, she was screaming, cursing his love of cars and all things speed. Whether it was pregnancy hormones running amok or not, each time she closed her eyes to sleep she was tormented by visions of worst-case scenarios.

This weekend was for them. It was to create memories to see them through their sleepless nights, to keep them smiling when the days were long and filled with trials. It was a chance to be young and reckless one last time before they became parents. Georgie was determined to make the most of it.

It was the final night of their long weekend. Billy and Georgie sat together on a double egg chair overlooking the lake. A plush blanket kept them warm against the early autumnal chill in the air.

Their days had been filled with massages, lounging on comfy beds beside an indoor pool, and reminiscing on their life together so far. It was a goodbye to the freedom of before, and hello to a challenge they would rise to together.

Georgie reached out for Billy's hand. She placed it on top of her smooth bump, moving it from place to place as the baby kicked and elbowed to make itself known. The action was second nature now, a routine they'd completed countless times. Billy's eyes filled with tears.

"What's wrong?" she asked, worried by the sudden change in his mood.

"It's just... in a few weeks, there will be three of us. We won't have quiet like this again. I thought I'd be more stressed about it, but all I feel is happiness. I want the chaos and the sleepless nights. I want the stinky nappies and the endless crying and everything else that comes with it. I want all of this as long as I have it with you."

Georgie's eyes tingled and began to collect unspent tears. She'd always known how much he loved her, how much he was looking forward to this baby. But to move him to this extent... it overwhelmed her.

"Feeling it like this is my favourite thing. Except for imagining our lives together. That makes my heart do cartwheels in my chest. I am *so* excited for what is to come."

"Me too, love. I've never been happier than I am now. The three of us, we can do anything. All we need is each other."

Georgie's hand moved Billy's to a new spot and the baby pounded it with kicks from within. They both laughed, encouraged by the ferocity of its movements.

"I think it's a boy. It's got to be with legs like that." Billy cooed over the bump, whispering sweet words of love to the baby. He'd told Georgie about how the child would be able to hear and know their voices by now. It had shocked her at first. But then, after the madness of pregnancy, she wasn't as surprised as perhaps she might have been.

Georgie fought to hide the smile that threatened to explode on her face at his words. Keeping the sex of the baby secret for over ten weeks now had been difficult. At times, she'd felt like telling him just so she could prepare things. Other times, she'd want to do so out of spite for the child that kept her up all night or made her heart race like she'd run a marathon rather than simply walked up the stairs. But she'd kept it.

In that perfect moment, with the sun setting and the scenery surrounding them, Georgie considered once more whether to tell him. It would be easy to accidentally-on-purpose slip up and agree with his statement. She held her tongue, though.

"Thank you," Billy said, resting his head against her shoulder.

"For what?" She raised an eyebrow and looked down to see him gazing adoringly at her.

"For not telling me. I know it's hard."

"Oh, you have no idea," she teased.

"I can imagine. But thank you also for giving me everything I've always wanted. You've given me a family, and I will never be able to repay you for that gift."

"Billy, what's got into you? You're soppier than a three-day-old piece of lettuce." Georgie wasn't used to this side of him, and it threw her. She was used to the goofy, happy-go-lucky Billy who cracked jokes about everything. Had the baby really changed him that much?

"I'm being serious now." He sat up, cupping her face and gently tugging it so she stared at him. "I love you with all my heart and soul. I love our baby too."

It wasn't just words. His sentiment swarmed the air,

choking Georgie with his sincerity. He stared deep into her eyes, his chestnut orbs delving deep into the mines of her being. She had no idea what he was looking for, but she hoped he saw the love she had for him reflected from within.

"I love you too. You've given me everything I've wished for. My home, you, this child. You are my everything. I am nothing without you."

Billy leaned in, delicately brushing his lips against hers. The sensation sent a tingle through her, sparking her senses and setting every nerve alight with passion. She opened her mouth, allowing him to deepen the kiss as his hands roamed over her bump, her chest, and the base of her neck. With a hand fisted in her long hair, Billy pressed her as close to him as her stomach would allow, moaning with need.

She broke off, looking at his lust-filled eyes. The darkened hue made her want more. Georgie giggled, an innocent sound that belied the sinful thoughts she enjoyed in her mind.

Billy was her world. She'd meant every word she'd spoken to him. She had never been happier, never felt more loved, or more full of love for those important people in her life—Billy and their unborn son. It grew, a weed of the best kind, invading every spare inch of her and rooting deep.

Only one thing played on her mind. How could she love another when her whole heart was consumed by Billy? Georgie didn't have long to wait until she'd find out, and it terrified her.

SEVEN

THE GUITAR RIFF OF FLEETWOOD MAC'S *THE CHAIN* DISTURBED Georgie's thoughts. She'd been pondering over Billy's name suggestions whilst she repacked her hospital bag again. Repeating her old mantra of 'if it's important, they'll call back', she continued to select her favourite outfits.

As it was their first child and they were short on friends and family, they'd spent a considerable sum picking out clothing. It was all freshly washed and neatly folded into the furniture they'd spent hours deciding on. The drawers and cot matched perfectly with the mint green walls Billy had painted a few weeks ago. Everything was ready.

Georgie had grown impatient, wanting the baby to come sooner. There were about seven weeks left, give or take a few days, but she knew first-time mums often went over. It was the one thing about all this she couldn't control—when the baby would arrive.

Georgie's phone rang again, and she huffed as she pushed herself off the floor to retrieve it. She really needed to stop sitting for so long in one position. It made her hips ache more than a normal day, and her knees creaked as she rose. They definitely didn't tell you things like this when they shared pregnancy tales.

The tones cut off just as she reached the handset and Georgie grumbled. *Always the way.* About to resume her activities, the phone rang again. The sudden noise jolted her and she almost dropped it. She accepted the call, relieved she'd managed to keep hold of it. Most things that ended up on the floor stayed there now.

"Hello?" she said, kicking herself for not checking the identity of the caller before she pressed accept. Knowing her luck, she'd end up having a chat with some pushy salesperson.

"Is this Miss Carpenter?" The voice on the other end was official, and there was a bustling background noise that made it hard to hear them properly.

"Yes, speaking." Georgie switched to her formal telephone voice she saved for clients.

"This is Geoff. I work with Billy."

"Okay. And how can I help you today, Geoff?"

"You might want to sit down."

Geoff's words made her blood run cold. Why would she need to sit down? Unless…

"What happened?" Georgie didn't want the answers, but she needed them.

"There was an accident on the track. Billy was… he was in the car doing the test run and he spun out. He's…"

Georgie didn't hear anything else. The phone dropped from her hand and each breath stabbed her in the ribs as she inhaled. Panting, she tried to get more oxygen into her system. It was no use. The room started to spin as she backed against the wall, sliding down until her bottom hit the floor.

"Miss Carpenter? Are you there?" She could hear the voice coming from the handset, but it didn't register. "Miss Carpenter, I need to know if you're okay. Please say something."

Shaking herself, Georgie reached out. She held the phone like it was a bomb, arm outstretched and hand shaking. With a flick of her thumb, she placed the call on speaker.

"I'm here." She couldn't say anything else. Her tongue was glued to the roof of her mouth, pinned in place by her heart, which felt like it was beating fast in her throat.

"I'm sorry, I know it's a shock. Can you drive, or do you need us to send someone?"

"Drive?"

"Yes, drive. To the hospital." Geoff spoke in short sentences. He must have thought she was a simpleton.

"I can't drive. My bump is too big."

Geoff gulped, the noise audible through the line. "Ah, yes. I'd forgotten how close you were. We'll send someone. They'll be there soon. In the meantime, try not to worry. Billy is in safe hands."

Georgie's brain was a jumbled mess. Why did she need to go so urgently if she wasn't meant to worry? It didn't make any sense. "I don't understand…" she said, but Geoff had already ended the call.

It could have been minutes or hours later when there was a sharp knock at the door. Georgie rose with difficulty from where she'd been sitting since taking the call and walked downstairs in a daze. Grabbing a coat and her handbag, she opened the door.

"Miss Carpenter?" She nodded and the thin man in front of her continued. "Great. Climb in. We'll get you to the hospital as fast as we can."

Blindly following, she sat on the back seat in silence, fiddling with her rings. When the car pulled onto the road, Georgie let a single tear fall. She wiped it away quickly. She needed to hold it together. Billy needed her to be strong. He'd need help with his recovery, but at least he'd be at home to spend time with their son when he arrived. And if he couldn't work for a while, she wouldn't have to worry about him missing the birth. *It was all going to be fine.*

Just over an hour later, the driver pulled up in the drop-off zone outside a hospital entrance. She hadn't paid attention for the whole journey, her mind filled with plans on how to make the house more comfortable for Billy whilst he recovered. At the very least, she'd need something to keep him occupied because if there was a long time out of the car, he was going to be unbearable.

Georgie had no idea where she was. A woman opened her door with a sad smile and held a hand out.

"Georgie? I'm Beth. I'll take you to Billy."

Refusing the hand, Georgie grabbed her things and followed Beth. The hospital was a mishmash of old and new, with glass everywhere but the usual ceiling tiles that were in every building like this.

They weaved through the corridors, through swinging doors, and up elevators until they came to a stop outside a private room. Beth froze, her eyes darting around as if she was looking for someone. A man in blue scrubs came round a corner and Beth's face softened in relief. An unspoken conversation appeared to take place as the man walked towards them.

"Miss Carpenter?" he asked.

"Yes. Where's Billy?" The need to see him burned fiercely within her. Being here, knowing she was this close, reignited it tenfold and Georgie struggled to remain polite.

"He's just through here. Before we go in, I should warn you his injuries are extensive. Billy is in a medically induced coma to ease the pressure on his brain. We don't know at this point if he will wake up." His voice was calm and kind, and his hazel eyes flickered to her prominent bump. "I'm sorry I don't have better news."

Georgie swallowed and clenched her fists to stop her hands from shaking. "Can I..." She stopped, inhaling deeply and staring at the ceiling. Her eyes prickled and her nose stung as she fought her emotions. "Can I see him?"

"Of course. Follow me." He opened the door in front of her and gentle beeping drifted through to the corridor. She breathed deeply again before she moved. Forcing her feet forward, Georgie stepped into the room.

Billy lay on the bed, bruises covering his bare chest and his face. If she hadn't known it was him, she wouldn't have recognised him. He was so broken. How could he ever recover from this? The little life inside her kicked hard. Did it know something she didn't?

"Oh, Billy," she whispered as she took a seat by his bed. Georgie reached out for his hand, taking it in hers and pulling it to her face. As she looked over his still body, she knew he wasn't waking up. No one, not even Billy, who had enough energy for three lifetimes, was returning from this.

EIGHT

Georgie sat, her hand periodically reaching up to wipe the tears that had been falling in an endless stream since they'd told her Billy wasn't going to wake up. She'd sat there, refusing to move, believing they were wrong. For three whole days, Georgie had spoken to Billy, told him he'd get better. She'd even perched on the bed so he could feel their child kicking. But it was no use.

No evidence of brain activity was how the doctors had explained it. It was the regular puff of air from the machines keeping him alive. Without the steady beep of the monitors and the dozens of tubes and wires, he'd already be cold.

With nothing more to be done, the doctors had asked her about organ donation and whether they could turn the machines off. Georgie hadn't responded the first time or the second. On the third time of asking, they'd pulled her outside and made her realise he wasn't coming back. There was no goodbye, not from him.

But she could have one. She'd signed the forms, agreeing they could take whatever organs could be useful to another. When they'd looked into it further, his body had been so damaged there was little they could use—his eyes, a kidney, and maybe some skin grafts from his legs, which had been mostly unscathed. It pained her to know he would be split into pieces like that, but he wouldn't need them.

The nurse and doctor entered the room. Their entrance sucked the air from her lungs and she choked on fresh tears. It was time.

"Five more minutes, please," she begged, not ready to say goodbye. Not yet.

The doctor nodded. "Take all the time you need. We'll be outside once you're ready." They exited, leaving her alone with Billy and a child that thrashed frantically inside her, fighting to be close to its father for the first and last time.

She exhaled, a ragged sound chasing the air from her lungs. Rubbing her stomach, she cooed at the child. It wouldn't stop. She reached for Billy's hand and placed it under hers, right on top of where the baby was making itself known.

"I don't want this to be real. I keep hoping I'm going to wake up and this is just one of those vivid pregnancy dreams. I want to tell you about it and hear you laugh. But I can't." She stopped, her chest heaving at the realisation she'd never hear his voice, his laugh ever again.

The baby stopped moving, so Georgie climbed on the bed and placed her head on Billy's chest. She took care of the wires, but she made herself comfortable. She'd not been able to stay on her side for long since the very early stages of her pregnancy. The last time they'd lay like this they'd been making plans for those first days of being parents. How different this situation was.

"It's a boy, you know. You're going to have a son." Her voice broke and she allowed her sorrow to wrap her in a sea of tears. "He'll never meet you, but he'll know you. He'll know all about your loves, and the things you hate. How you make stupid jokes about everything. How you can't even cook cheese on toast. I'll make sure he knows you.

"All those things we planned, we'll do them. You might not be there in person, but we'll take your picture, your memory—you'll come everywhere with us. He will feel your love through the veil.

"A boy, Billy. We're having a boy." Saying it aloud made it more real. Georgie would have to teach him all of those things Billy should have covered. Peeing standing up—how would she even begin with that one?

She looked down at the bruised hand beneath hers and beyond it to the kicks that were visible to the naked eye. The baby was going wild. Did it know its daddy was dying? That this was its last chance to be near him?

Georgie had so much more to say, but she couldn't get the words out. They lodged in her throat, choking her. The ones that did make it into the room smothered her, cutting off her air with the pain they caused.

"It was never supposed to be this way, was it? We always said whatever happens, but this wasn't…." She squeezed his hand and stroked his cheek. "We were supposed to rule the world—you, me, and the family we created. We're alone now, me and him. All alone. You might watch over us, but you're not going to be here. You won't take the slack when he's sick in the night or do an emergency nappy run. It's just me."

It was selfish of her to think that way. Billy wouldn't go if he could help it. He had been excited for this baby. He was the one with all the baby books, the names…

A name.

The errant thought led to another and she knew the child's name. It was the only thing it could be. Georgie smiled, despite the sadness clawing at the threads holding her together.

"Sebastian Billy McIntyre. How does that sound, love?"

The silence cut deep. He'd been so excited about names, but she'd not even thought of them. It felt right to go with

Billy's favourite—a way to connect him to the baby once it arrived.

Georgie lifted her head, pushing up to rest on her elbows so she could watch the rise and fall of Billy's chest. See his beautiful face once more. The purple splotches hid his rosy cheeks and the swollen lids caged his bright brown eyes, but if she closed her own, she could see them.

Moving his hand so it rested on her cheek, she succumbed to the sobs that had lingered in the shadows of her heart. The closer they came to saying goodbye, the harder it got. She wanted to scream and shout and smash everything she could touch. She wanted him to wake up. Anything. That was what she'd give.

It didn't matter, though. He was gone.

Finally, she controlled the wrenching sobs and sat up. Georgie took one last look at Billy's shell before sliding off the bed and walking into the corridor. Within three steps of leaving the room she'd called home for the last four days, she collapsed to the floor. Grief made her feet cement blocks. Loss turned her joints to stone.

It wasn't meant to be like this.

But it was.

THE BLACK DRESS WAS TIGHT OVER HER STOMACH, SEAMS FIT TO burst if she bent the wrong way. She'd gone for a slick bun and forgone makeup around her honey eyes. Billy had always said she didn't need it.

Stillness reigned. In her routine, she moved to a new room and stayed in one place. The baby had slowed down, but it was nothing concerning. After a panicked dash to the maternity triage, she'd found it was her lack of eating causing the problem. They'd given her a good talking to, probably flagged her on some system too. Georgie made sure to eat from then on, but only for him. She wanted to be in the void with Billy.

A knock on the door disturbed her quiet and she looked around, about to ask Billy to get it to save her walking downstairs. But he couldn't. She gulped air and fought to stop the tears that were always forcing their way through. Sometimes, she cried and didn't even know tears were falling until she felt the wetness soak through Billy's shirt. Wearing his clothes numbed the pain, but only a little.

When she didn't answer, the person knocked again. She waddled down the stairs and sighed when she opened it. A gentleman in a black top hat and tailcoat stood before her. He held a cane and when Georgie looked beyond him, she could see the hearse and Billy.

The mahogany coffin had just two sets of flowers atop. It was an arrangement of his name from her and a small race car from the baby. She'd debated having 'daddy', but even the word cut her open and left her emotions bleeding. No, a reminder today of what he was missing, what she wouldn't get, was too much.

"We're ready when you are, Miss Carpenter."

Georgie nodded and followed the man to the car, only locking up when he prompted her to. Her head felt like she'd shoved it into a goldfish bowl—she saw everything, but all the sounds were muffled. It was easier that way.

Opting for the family car had been an indulgence, but Georgie had no one else to drive her and she wasn't able to drive herself. Being an only child, like Billy, had been something they'd bonded over, but with both of their parents dying young and their wider family being estranged, it left her isolated on a day when she would have given anything to have someone with her.

This was one of those times she regretted her choice to move away, to keep people at a distance. All she'd needed was Billy, he was her world. But now her world was gone.

Colleagues of both her and Billy were waiting outside the church, whispering kind words that she never heard. They fell into step behind her as she walked alone behind his coffin. It was the hardest thing she'd had to do, but she knew in a few short weeks she'd have much worse to cope with—she would be giving birth without her soulmate to support her.

Numbness enveloped her as she took a seat on the front pew. The service washed over her, touching her but not seeping in. Georgie nodded in the right places, looked at the right messages on cards, shook the right hands, but nothing was right. It was all wrong. All horribly, painfully wrong.

When she got home from the small wake the funeral directors had arranged, she let her mask fall. The salty tears cascaded down her cheeks once more as she pulled Billy's favourite shirt over her head and climbed into his side of the bed. Wishing for oblivion to come but wanting to live for their child was exhausting, and she was done with it.

NINE

Checking the time on her phone, Georgie groaned. Two minutes past one. Not even an hour had passed since she had last checked it moments before she'd dropped off. Sleep was difficult anyway, thanks to her overly large stomach and aching hips. Since Billy, it was even harder to find peaceful rest.

A sharp twinge in her side made her wince, but she shrugged it off. It must have been a pulled muscle from how she'd fallen asleep. Knowing it would be hard to get back to sleep, Georgie stretched and headed for the kitchen. A hot chocolate would help relax her, even if it flared her heartburn in return.

Must be a hairy baby. She heard Billy's jokey tone in her head. He'd teased her relentlessly that she must be carrying Chewbacca with the amount of Gaviscon she was chugging daily. It was a load of old wives' tales, but the longer the pregnancy went on, the worse it got. She was struck with a desire to talk about it with him. Loneliness clawed at her; she was the mouse in the paws of a fickle cat that took pleasure in playing with her emotions.

As she waited for the kettle to boil, Georgie walked to the fridge. She didn't want anything, but it was her habit to scan the fridge for treats. This week's fruit drawing was missing from the calendar. The gap in the little box was a gut punch.

A deep moan came from her. Billy had been drawing a comical picture each week. They'd made her smile despite everything, but he'd never gone more than a couple of weeks in advance. He hadn't wanted to tempt fate, he'd said.

Pouring the hot water into the cup, she stirred with one hand whilst opening her baby tracker app. A romaine lettuce. Georgie laughed despite herself at the thought of Billy drawing that.

"I miss you," she whispered, hugging his fleece dressing gown tight around her. She grabbed her cup and walked slowly back to bed, a moan escaping her lips as each step sent stabbing pains through her lower back.

A second twinge, like the one that had woken her, caught Georgie off guard when she reached the bedroom door. She gasped, the sudden pain making her hands jolt. Cursing, she sucked the hot liquid off her fingers and climbed into bed. She didn't have the energy or the inclination to clean the mess on the floor. Or the house in general for that matter. Nesting had totally passed her by.

With a sigh, Georgie flicked on the TV and scrolled through to the next episode of the show she'd been watching. It was an easy-to-follow drama she barely paid attention to. She'd seen it before but she needed something in the background. The quiet in the house, the empty feeling it had, was the worst.

Georgie imagined each little noise she heard was Billy pottering around. It wasn't—she knew that—but she couldn't bring herself to admit he was gone. She didn't want to accept that she was about to become a solo parent.

Her stomach continued to cramp every so often, but she

ignored it. Georgie had been having feelings like this on and off for days. Trusty Doctor Google said it was just Braxton Hicks, so she wasn't worried. The baby would come when it was ready, but her body was just making sure she was prepared.

She relaxed back onto the mountain of pillows and sipped at her drink. The combination of exhaustion, hot chocolate, and background noise helped lull Georgie into a light sleep.

"Ouch," she cried out. A particularly painful squeeze in her stomach took her breath.

The TV was quiet, waiting for her to confirm she was still watching. The early strains of the birdsong alarm clock crept in through the curtains. When the pain subsided, she grabbed her phone, and the realisation she'd dropped off again clicked into place. It was nearly dead, so she pushed herself out of the lush king-size bed to put it on charge.

As she bent to get the cable, another sharp pain made Georgie gasp, and she needed a moment to return to a standing position. It was the strongest she'd felt yet and she began to question her belief—were these really Braxton Hicks? The baby wasn't quite due yet; there were a few weeks until her expected date, but she knew any time after thirty-seven weeks would be seen as safe.

Georgie felt a wave of panic rise and fall within her stomach. What if these were contractions? She'd barely processed losing Billy; she needed time to prepare to be a parent. Pacing, she pulled up her internet app and searched for descriptions of contractions. Her finger flicked through the results, skimming the first few lines before exhaling loudly.

It's time, baby. Our son is coming. For the second time in less than twenty-four hours, Georgie heard Billy speaking to her. Was the impending labour sending her a little tapped in the head? It didn't matter; she knew in her heart the imaginary Billy was right—these weren't Braxton Hicks.

Georgie changed her search term and pulled up the number for the local hospital. Saving it to her phone along with a taxi firm, she walked around the bedroom rubbing her lower back and waiting for the next contraction. It didn't take long to come and they quickly established a pattern. Not close enough to warrant a call… yet. But they were strong enough to leave her raiding her cupboards for paracetamol and running a hot bath in the hopes it might ease the aches.

Slipping slightly, thanks to a sharp pain as she stepped into the bath, Georgie threw an arm out and managed to save herself on the towel rail. Anger rose within her. Billy should be here, helping her settle her nerves and massaging oils into her back like they'd planned. He was meant to be timing things on the app he'd downloaded specially for it.

"I'm not ready," she moaned, rocking back and forth in the water. It did little to help, so she climbed back out and wrapped herself in a towel. Throwing on old joggers in case her waters went, Georgie paired it with an oversized tee and threw her wet hair into a scruffy bun.

Her heart throbbed in her chest, accelerating each time there was another sign the baby was coming. She screamed and fought the tears that so desperately wanted to fall. Truth be told, Georgie was petrified. Giving birth was scary when you had a loved one by your side, but she was alone. Not just because her partner was away with work, but because he was dead. This was just the first step in a long, lonely, difficult journey and she didn't want to take it.

The longer the contractions went on, the more drained Georgie became. Her breath came in ragged pants and cries between crushing sensations around her stomach. It was like no pain she'd ever experienced, but it still didn't come close to the agony she felt in her heart every time she thought of Billy.

You can do this, baby. Call them.

Whether she was going mad or there was a way of

communicating beyond the grave, she wasn't sure. But Billy was right. With just a few minutes between contractions and each one now lasting around a minute, she needed to get checked.

"Hello? I think I need to come and have my baby," she said, rushing the sentence because she knew another wave of pain was due any second.

"All right, my sweet. Can I have your name?"

"Ge—aaah—sorry. Georgie Carpenter," she gasped.

"That's all right. Just breathe through the pain and take your time. When did your contractions start?" the friendly midwife asked. She had a calm voice and it made Georgie feel a tiny bit less isolated. Just a tiny bit, though.

"Last night, about two a.m., I think." Georgie glanced at the bedside cabinet and noticed she'd likely been in labour for at least fifteen hours, possibly more. Each second had dragged, but she was surprised how long she had coped on her own. It buoyed her, giving her an injection of energy when she needed it most.

"Okay. And how often are they?"

"Every few minutes." Georgie wanted to keep things brief so she could get answers before the next one hit.

"And how long do they last?"

"About a minute, sometimes longer. Please, I'm on my own." She felt pitiful, but this short conversation had shown her it was time to stop being stubborn. Pretending it wasn't happening wasn't going to slow the baby's arrival. He was coming today, or maybe tomorrow, and she needed to accept that.

"Okay, my sweet. If you want to make your way up to the maternity department as soon as you can. We're on the second floor. Take a left out of the elevator and walk right to the end. We'll get you checked and decide what is going to be best."

Georgie whispered her thanks, dropping the phone as she

succumbed to yet another excruciating pain around her bump. She waited for the haze to fade before she called a taxi and bounced her bags down the stairs.

"I need you, Billy," she moaned to the empty house. "I need you."

TEN

Georgie looked at the small bundle in the plastic cot next to her. He wriggled in his sleep, throwing his arms out suddenly before opening his eyes slowly. She should love him, she knew she should.

But she couldn't.

The baby drew breath, its tiny lungs filling, ready to scream again. It was all he seemed to do. Nothing she did was good enough. Nothing she did could soothe the creature's woes. Woes so great for one so small.

After ignoring him for as long as she could, she lifted the child to her breast gingerly. Wincing as he latched, Georgie turned her gaze to the ceiling, silent tears leaving tracks on her tired face.

The instant bond, the amazing connection she was supposed to feel wasn't there. She couldn't care less if one of the other mothers in the ward grabbed him in the night and fed him for her. After four days stuck in one room with strangers and their wailing brats, she was done.

Four days, and already she knew motherhood wasn't for her. Already she knew, regardless of how happy everyone else was over the child's arrival, she couldn't love him. Not when he was a reminder of him.

He had Billy's nose, his smile, even his short temper. But he wasn't him. Billy would never hold him, never help in the night to soothe him. He would always be just a reminder of what should have been. What wouldn't be.

Someday she might love him. Somehow it might be all right. But not right now.

It was such a contradiction to how she'd felt all those years ago in Mrs Barber's classroom. Billy's cruel laughter at her desire to be a mummy had cut her deep, but not as much as doing it without him did. He had been the one who'd been excited. He'd been the one making plans for the baby when it was just a word on a screen. Georgie had been petrified of failing—something she'd hidden from everyone.

The memory of Billy tipped her over the edge, and the tears she'd been sitting on since the baby arrived flooded down her face. She felt them crashing onto her exposed breast, saw them disturbing the child, but she couldn't stop.

"Oh, pet," came the sympathetic voice of a midwife who'd picked the wrong time to do her observations.

Georgie hadn't seen this one before. It meant she would have to explain their circumstances to someone new. She sniffed and tried to regain some control.

"Don't fuss on my account. Baby blues catch everyone around now, especially first-timers like yourself. They'll pass as soon as things settle, they always do. Here," she said, passing Georgie a tissue. "Where's little one's daddy? Is he not coming to visit today?"

The friendly smile vanished as the woman noticed Georgie's face. Fresh tears fell and a cry of heartbreak filled the curtained space. The midwife leaned over and pressed the call button before placing an arm around Georgie's shaking form.

"We need a side room preparing, please," she ordered,

and the woman who'd answered the alert shuffled off. "Now, let's have a chat, shall we?"

Georgie nodded. It was all she could do. The midwife went to take the now sleeping child from her arms, but Georgie held tight. It was the first time she'd felt a connection to the baby—she needed him close. For now, at least.

Holding her hands in an open gesture of surrender, the midwife took a seat on the edge of the bed. Georgie looked at her properly for the first time. Her tunic was darker than the others and she lacked the fresh face of most staff on the ward. Georgie assumed she must be a more senior midwife.

"I'm Tegan, and I'm the midwife in charge today. I'm sorry my question upset you. There was nothing in your notes about baby's dad being a sensitive topic for you. No one mentioned it at handover, either. I'll make sure that's fixed after our conversation."

Georgie swallowed. "It's okay. You didn't know." She watched the tiny chest rise and fall, the startle reflexes. Saying it aloud never did any good, so Georgie put it off for as long as she could.

"Know what, pet?" Tegan prompted when the silence had lingered for too long.

Eyes gazing into the harsh lighting on the ceiling, Georgie exhaled loudly before she spoke. "He's dead."

Tegan's face grew pale and her eyes popped wide for an instant before she controlled her reaction. "I'm so sorry, Georgie." She stopped for a moment before continuing, "Is there anyone else who will be around to help?"

"No, it's just me and…" Georgie trailed off. She'd still not managed to say his name. Even straight after he'd been born, she'd pretended she hadn't decided yet. He'd been Baby Carpenter for the best part of a week. Billy would have been fuming at her for not using the name they'd picked, not to mention forgetting to correct his surname to McIntyre.

"You and this little one. What's his name?" Tegan asked,

glancing at the whiteboards above the bed and the notes she had in her pocket.

"Sebastian," she whispered. A flash of love sparked within her but was gone in seconds, chased away by the stormy winds of numbness.

"Sebastian, eh? That's a sweet name. It suits him."

"Thank you. His dad picked it. He named him after his favourite racing driver. Well, second favourite. I vetoed Fernando." The first real smile she'd had since before she had taken that call pulled at her lips. It was tiny and fleeting, but it still felt so wrong. How could she smile when he wasn't here to enjoy it with her?

"Well, Georgie, we're going to get you settled into a side room on your own so you can get some rest," Tegan said, standing and brushing the creases out of her tunic. "Is it okay if I pull some information together for you?" Tegan's kindly smile had returned and she bustled about taking her blood pressure and temperature. She checked Sebastian too, declaring him perfectly healthy despite his early appearance.

Georgie had no idea what information she might be able to provide that she couldn't find on Google, but she nodded anyway. "Some sleep would be helpful, I guess." She shrugged, the short moment of sensation, connection with another human fading. It was always this way. She was a radio that couldn't hold a signal, forever cutting out.

Tegan laughed. "Sleep is always hard in this place, but Sebastian here seems to know how to do it, so you might as well make the most of it whilst you can. Besides, if you're ever going to get out of here, we need to get that blood pressure under control. Sleep deprivation won't help."

Georgie mumbled her thanks as she placed the baby back into the plastic cot. The teddy Billy had picked after their twenty-week scan—a small red bull—was tucked into the bottom.

He'd had so many plans and dreams for this little guy.

None of them would happen now. Fresh emotions surged but anger was the driving force this time.

Tegan seemed to sense the change in energy. "If you gather everything up, we'll move you in a few minutes." She left with a small smile. Pulling the curtain behind her, Tegan gave Georgie space to be alone with her thoughts.

The distraction packing brought was welcome and helped Georgie to control her feelings. But only just. The clothes and toiletries took the brunt of her frustration as she threw them into her case.

Conflict ate away at her. The rage was focused on one person. The person the baby looked like. The person who'd abandoned her with a newborn.

Why did he have to leave?

It was a question she'd never get an answer to, but it didn't stop her asking it multiple times a day.

ELEVEN

AFTER A WEEK OF BEING STUCK IN THE HOSPITAL, GEORGIE AND Sebastian were finally settling into some sort of routine back at home. He screamed, she fed him, rocked him, changed him, then he'd sleep and the cycle would start again. Endless nights, neverending days, and whilst she was now never alone, Georgie felt lonelier than ever.

Even on the nights he slept, Georgie was awake, watching him and wishing Billy was with them. Every day was a chore and she frequently skipped self-care tasks like showering or dressing herself because she couldn't be bothered. No one saw her except Sebastian, and he didn't care what she looked like as long as she shoved a boob in his mouth multiple times a day.

As the days went on, the bond she'd expected still wasn't developing. It felt just as alien having Sebastian in a crib next to her bed as it did when she first found out she was pregnant. There was no joy in the tiny things he did, no pleasure in seeing his little fingers wrap around hers or the adoring way he stared up at her whenever she scooped him up for another feed. All she saw was Billy, and that reminded her of what she was missing.

She'd made an effort this morning on account of the midwife being due. Because of her overlong stay and her lack of support, she'd earned the sympathy of some—or maybe concern for Sebastian's safety—so they'd been holding off discharging her fully. Georgie was hopeful today would be the day. She'd healed as much as it was possible to, Sebastian was healthy, and the constant intrusion of strangers into their world was unwanted. Caring for him was a chore. Like the washing up; it had to be done.

The door knocked and a new midwife laden with bags and weighing scales bustled into the room with a smile. "Hi! You must be Georgie. I'm Holly. How are you both doing today?" Her eyes scanned the room and lingered on the dead flowers next to the photos of Billy. It was a shrine of sorts Georgie had created and maintained before Sebastian had arrived. Now she had no energy for it.

Georgie stifled a yawn. "Yes, that's me. We're fine, thank you."

"Little one keeping you up?" The friendly expression twitched with concern, but she said nothing.

"Mmhmm." Georgie was non-committal, having already learned sometimes less was more.

Holly went about her checks, weighing Sebastian, asking questions about his feeding, his nappies, and Georgie's wellbeing. Georgie breezed through them, lying about herself but being honest about Sebastian.

Tell her the truth. Billy's voice invaded her thoughts again and she shook her head.

Leave me alone, she snapped back. *You left me. Left us. You don't get a say in how we do things, not anymore.*

"Are you all right?" Holly asked, her brows furrowing as she reached out to put her hand over Georgie's.

"Yes, all fine, thank you. Just tired."

"It's really hard, especially when you're on your own." She rummaged in her bag and passed Georgie a leaflet.

SOMEDAY

Postnatal Depression
What is it and when to seek help

Georgie recoiled from the piece of paper, her face contorting with disgust. "I don't need that. I'm not depressed."

"I'm not saying you are, lovely. But I always make a point of leaving one with mums in your situation. These emotions can creep up on anyone, even when they don't have such…" Holly paused and searched for a word. "…heartbreak surrounding the arrival of a baby." When Georgie still refused to take it, Holly left it on the sofa, typed something on her laptop, and quickly buckled up her bag.

Remembering her manners, Georgie stood and escorted Holly to the door. "Thank you."

"You're welcome. Don't discount that leaflet. It might have things that can help you." With a sad smile, she left Georgie and Sebastian. Alone again. Always alone.

GETTING DRESSED, PACKING A NAPPY BAG, AND FIGURING OUT the pushchair took more energy than Georgie had that morning. She'd spent the night imagining life with Billy still here rather than sleeping. The fact Sebastian had his newborn check at the doctors' had completely slipped her very chaotic mind.

They'd barely made it on time, and she stared at the opposite wall in the waiting room. People cooed over the six-week-old in the pram, but Georgie gave polite nods. Her baby was beautiful, but he was also too like his father. Looking at him more than she had to made her chest compact and breathing became difficult.

When her name was called, she rose and pushed Sebastian into the little consulting room. A familiar face greeted her.

Doctor Pike had been looking after her since she was a little girl. He'd sorted her out when her acne flared, and when she'd fallen to pieces after the loss of her parents. Relief, however fleeting, was a welcome change to the constant void Georgie had been living in.

"Congratulations, Georgie. Let's have a look at this little chap, shall we?" Doctor Pike was probably being over-familiar, but Georgie didn't mind. He was one of the closest things to family she had now. The thought cheered her and depressed her at the same time.

The doctor reached over and took the sleeping bundle in his experienced hands. He fussed over him, talking about how handsome he was and how he was sorry to poke him around like this. Georgie watched, interested in the checks taking place but not overly bothered by the outcome.

It was hard for her to explain. She didn't want Sebastian to be ill, but she lacked the energy to be concerned by each little thing she assumed most other new parents would be panicking over. They were the sorts of things Billy would have been checking at all hours. The thought of him stopped her short. He'd have been a better parent than she was. He was the one who'd been excited.

"He's a little champ, isn't he? Flying colours! His head control is very advanced, and he's an alert chap. But we need to check you over as well." The doctor's report broke Georgie from her toxic thought loop.

Once satisfied with Sebastian, the doctor's attention shifted. Georgie answered his questions about the birth, had her blood pressure checked, and had a chat about contraception. Not that she needed that.

"And how are you coping?" Doctor Pike asked, throwing a gaze at Georgie, which made her think the man knew she wasn't 'right'.

"Honestly?" Georgie snorted. "How do you think? I'm alone all the time with a baby I wasn't even that excited for.

This is the first time I've left the house since we came home, and the time before that was only to go to the hospital or my partner's funeral."

Doctor Pike nodded but didn't say anything. But now she'd started to tell the truth about her mental wellbeing, she couldn't stop.

"I don't feel anything. No pride, happiness, not even sadness. I'm just numb. I'm angry because Billy isn't here, but then I'm angry at the baby because he looks so much like him. But mostly, I'm tired. I don't sleep, I barely eat, and I don't even know if I…"

"If you what?" Doctor Pike prodded her for an answer after a considerable silence.

Tears welled in Georgie's eyes as she thought about what she was about to say. It was a cruel thing, but it was the truth. "I don't know if I love him." She jerked her head towards Sebastian. He was the perfect child. He slept well, didn't grumble too much, and filled the house with pleasant baby noises. "He deserves better. He needs his daddy."

She broke down, chest heaving in a way she hadn't experienced since the immediate aftermath of Billy's death. Doctor Pike handed her a tissue and waited for her to calm down.

"When I saw your name for the baby checks today, I wanted to see you myself. The midwife team flagged some concerns about your mental health, so I hoped you'd be more honest with me. Thank you for sharing that, Georgie." He reached out and patted Georgie's hand.

"I don't know what to do," Georgie whispered. Whilst she felt like the worst mother in the world, the weight she had been carrying for the last few weeks melted. Telling someone had brought a deep relief.

"Holly said she left a leaflet with you. Did you read it?"
"Yes."
"I think she was right. I think you're struggling with lots

of things. The changes of being a mother, your grief… I think you may have postnatal depression. If you'll let me, I'd like to arrange for some counselling and see if we can get you joined up to some mum and baby groups they run in the local community centre. The company will help you feel less isolated and usually, you'll find getting out of the house helps with the symptoms you're experiencing."

Georgie sat quietly. She'd always been independent, always wanted to survive on her own. But she couldn't do this alone. Not this time.

With a deep exhale, she spoke. "What do I need to do?"

TWELVE

DOCTOR PIKE HAD ARRANGED EVERYTHING. GEORGIE HAD dropped a box of cupcakes in for him as a thank you. It wasn't exactly healthy, but it was all she could think of with her tiredness growing worse by the day.

She'd refused medication, not wanting to jeopardise Sebastian's breastfeeding journey. Georgie knew from her studies how beneficial it was, plus, in her eyes, it was the lazy way. No sterilising, no getting the right formula and measuring things out—all she had to do was nudge a boob in his direction and he was happy. It would take longer, perhaps, but she had to put Sebastian first.

Even so, her symptoms had plateaued, but she still felt like a vacuum of emotion. Nothing came close enough to stir her dormant heart. Not even the gurgles and adoring glances of Sebastian came close to waking her from her numbness.

A few weeks ago, a letter inviting Georgie to her first counselling session landed on the doormat. She'd stared at it whilst eating breakfast one-handed as she fed Sebastian. It wasn't until he went down for his afternoon nap that she'd managed to gather enough courage to open it.

Now, it was time for her first session. She'd considered

cancelling, but Sebastian deserved better. Besides, Billy wouldn't have wanted her shuffling through life with her eyes closed. He'd always been one to grab an opportunity and run with it. She owed it to Sebastian to show him how exciting life could be.

Georgie approached the doctors' surgery where her counsellor was based. Her eyes flitted around the entrance, searching for any excuse not to enter. Once inside, she forced herself to inhale for three before exhaling for five to keep herself calm—it was a strategy she'd read about online. It didn't help.

Sebastian had fallen asleep on the walk there, and Georgie hoped he would stay that way throughout the session. When her name was called, she dropped her phone. She wasn't usually this easily flustered. The thought of baring all to a stranger was nightmare-inducing, giving her another contender for the top cause of sleep deprivation.

Once she was settled, she looked around the space. It was much like a standard consulting room, but it had a more comfortable-looking chair and no bed in the corner. Her counsellor sat with his hands clasped in his lap over a notebook, his leather-brown eyes observing her.

"Welcome. You can call me Leo," he said. He struck her as a man who was happy in his own company. Someone who could sit in silence and have more impact than if he spoke for an hour. It was daunting being opposite him.

"Thanks. I'm Georgie. Am I doing this right?" The whole situation felt bizarre to her.

"The first thing I'd like you to embrace is the idea that in this room, there is no right or wrong. There are truths, there are emotions, there are things you'll find difficult to talk about. That's all normal, and this is a safe space. You tell me what you want, when you want. I'll help you unpick that and help you with strategies to aid you in coping when you're on your own." Leo smiled, a kindly gesture that reached his eyes.

"Okay… it's just… this is all really new to me."

"It's often new to everyone who comes through those doors. That's normal. Why don't you start by telling me why you think you're here?"

Silence weighed on Georgie as she considered his question. She rocked Sebastian as he slept in his pushchair. It wasn't needed—he was still enjoying blissful dreams—but it calmed her, distracted her.

"I'm broken," she whispered, breathing deep before she continued. "I lost my partner, my best friend, my life. I don't know how to cope without him and because the baby looks so much like his dad, I can't even look at him. I'm a failure as a mother."

"Is he fed? Clean? Warm?" Leo asked. Georgie nodded with a frown. "Then you aren't a failure. I barely know you, but you're catering to his needs right now, even if you don't realise it consciously. Let me guess, you figured out movement helps him sleep, which is why you're rocking him?"

Georgie's eyebrows pulled together. "How did… Yes, he does. I hadn't thought of it like that."

"That's the aim of this—to change those negative thought patterns. It won't fix things overnight, but it will get better with time. All I ask is commitment and honesty. So, let's get started."

Before she knew it, Georgie was walking home in a daze. The session had been intense, but in the best way. The biggest revelation she'd had, although it wasn't really that surprising, was her failure to grieve for Billy. She'd never said goodbye, not properly. She'd always been waiting for him to come back.

Leo had set her some homework—to visit Billy's grave. Billy

had never wanted anything ostentatious, but there was a little plaque that had been erected at his resting place. Deciding there was no time like the present, Georgie double-checked she had enough nappies and spare clothes before heading to the bus stop.

Sebastian was awake by the time she arrived, but she was determined to face her problems head-on. Her session with Leo had awoken a fierceness inside her. Georgie was a survivor; she needed to get better.

She scooped the baby out of the pushchair and cradled him close. Sitting on the damp grass, she didn't even try to stop the tears that fell. With a movement that came as second nature, Georgie swivelled the little form so he was perched in the crook of her elbow, looking towards the plastic plaque that marked Billy's spot.

Billy wouldn't have wanted this. He was the one who had wanted this baby so badly. That wasn't to say she hadn't, but he'd been excited from the first test. She'd been scared, reluctant to be a parent. He should have been here.

It should have been her in that box. Her that had left him alone to navigate being a single parent and a widower before he was thirty. He'd have been better at it, especially after every book and parenting blog he read in those early weeks. He was the strong one.

This was the first time she'd given herself permission to feel this. It was freeing, letting the toxicity that had poisoned her for so long seep into the soil beneath her. It was like Billy was reaching out, shouldering the burden the only way he knew how. The only way he could—being a safe space for her like he'd always been.

A tiny ray of sunshine broke through the grey skies that had smothered the country for months. The beam of light from the heavens grew stronger, brighter, illuminating Sebastian's face, making the cobalt flecks in his eyes stand out. His eyes were the only thing that weren't like his dad and Georgie hoped they'd stay that way.

"We miss you, Billy." Georgie looked up to the clouds, beyond, to the sunlight forcing itself through. "Do you miss us? Do you see us?" The bundle in her arms wriggled, trying to hide from the sudden brightness. Georgie cooed at him, feeling more maternal in that moment than she'd felt in his eleven weeks of life. But it was fleeting, and before long, she was back to wondering what she was doing.

"You and your stupid cars. I should have made you stop as soon as we found out about Sebastian. Should have banned you from driving. It's your fault we're alone. Your fault he'll grow up without you."

The anger came from nowhere, bubbling like lava and spilling over in cruel words. Deep down, Georgie knew it had been an accident. But she didn't care. It needed to be said, needed an exit. Leo was right. It would be a long journey, but at least she'd made a start.

THE GOOD DAYS WERE STILL FEW BUT THERE WERE GOOD DAYS. That was what Georgie focused on, and she squeezed every second of positive energy from those. She'd noticed a difference in Sebastian too. Whether it was just her being more open to his interactions, or whether it was him responding better now she engaged with him, she didn't know. But she loved the change it had brought about in him.

All the baby sites said he wouldn't smile properly until around fourteen weeks, but Georgie was certain he was doing it early. The strange sense of maternal pride filled her every time he gave it a go. It felt peculiar, almost like the aftermath of pins and needles—necessary, but not unwelcome.

Today was a good day, and she was joining in with the peek-a-boo and the silly noises, trying to encourage that elusive first proper smile. Right on cue, Sebastian filled his second nappy of the day, and she felt the familiar wave of disappointment take control. Georgie carried him to the changing mat and laid him down on it. She forced a smile as she dealt with the offensive-smelling downside of a baby. Her focus was so streamlined on making sure he was clean that she almost missed it.

"Oh my gosh! Do it again, baby boy. Smile for Mummy!" Georgie cooed over him. The force of the happiness took her by surprise and tears pricked at her eyes. "Yes, that's it, keep going!"

It was as Sebastian's perfect cupid bow lips curved upwards into the cutest expression she'd ever seen that Georgie realised his eyes weren't looking at her. She tracked his vision—he was gazing over her shoulder. Straight at Billy's picture. The happiness was crushed in an instant, replaced by the weight of their loss. Billy missed his first real milestone.

I saw it.

Georgie jumped and stared around. The room was empty, but she could have sworn she heard Billy's voice. It was the first time since she'd started going to counselling, and the first time on a good day too.

"Billy?" she said, instantly regretting it. Of course he wasn't there. Silence answered her, but little Sebastian continued staring over her shoulder. It was like he was playing with someone. Georgie rocked back to sit on her heels and watched him.

A sudden burst of clarity hit her in the chest. The force of it took her breath, but as the initial sensation faded, a knowledge—certainty—hit her. Billy was gone. He wasn't coming back. But Sebastian was real, he was here, and she had to be there for these tiny moments. For her, for him, for Billy. It was progress, however small, and she couldn't wait to build on it.

EPILOGUE

Seeing Sebastian in his dark blue school jumper and grey trousers brought tears to Georgie's eyes. He looked so grown up, so smart. His cheeky smile—the image of his dad's—melted her. God help his teacher. The kid knew just how to push the limits without stepping out of line. Another trait he'd inherited from Billy.

"Seb, say cheese for Mummy, darling."

"Cheeeeseeee." The toothy grin was adorable. This image was a keeper. It would join the wall with photos of his first day at nursery, getting his first shoes, his first meals… all things they'd done together. All things his dad had missed.

"Have you got your photo of Daddy?"

"Yes, Mummy. He in my pocket. He safe there."

"Good. He'll look after you today, just like he always does." She swallowed the lump she always got in her throat when she talked about Billy.

Georgie stepped forward and kissed his head, breathing deeply the fruity shampoo he picked himself. Her baby wasn't a baby anymore. Squeezing him tight, she looked over at the photos of Billy gazing down at them. *I hope I've done you proud.*

Even after five years, the pain was still fresh. But thanks to the support of a grief counsellor, the mum and baby group she'd joined, and the new friends she'd made when she retrained as a counsellor herself, she was coping. Being able to help others through what she'd struggled with and caring for her son made each day worth living.

They talked about Billy every day. Seb said good morning and goodnight to his little photo, taking it everywhere with him. She dreaded the day someone teased him for it, but she'd face that when it came. He was a strong boy, much stronger than her, and she saw so much of Billy in him. It was a blessing most days.

"Come on, or we'll be late on your first day."

Securing the Velcro on his shoes, she grabbed his coat, book bag, and juice bottle as she pulled the door behind her. Seb waited patiently on the drive, chewing at his lip whilst he did.

"Mummy, do I have to go to school? I want to stay with you and Daddy."

"You'll have a wonderful time. You'll make new friends, have lots of fun, and you'll forget all about Mummy for a while. I promise." She hugged him tight, grabbing his hand to begin the short walk to school.

She'd moved here specifically, wanting the familiarity of the school she and Billy went to for their son. That and the fact she hadn't the heart to live in the house they'd built virtually from scratch together. Each room held memories of them chipping off plaster or flicking paint at each other. It was too much.

The walk was familiar and filled with parents. Some smiled sadly, others looked relieved to be able to have respite from their children for a few hours. Georgie was a chaotic mess. She wanted Seb to go to school, but it was another first without the man she'd intended to spend her life with.

When the teacher walked out, Georgie's face split into a

bright smile. "You'll be in safe hands with this teacher. She's one of the best." She looked down on Seb's little face, watching him stare at the older woman in front of him.

"Georgie Carpenter? You've not changed a bit. And who is this young man?"

"Thank you, Mrs Barber. You're too kind." She nudged the child forward. "Say hello."

"Hello," said Sebastian. The women both laughed.

"What's your name?"

"Sebastian Billy McIntyre. My daddy picked it."

"He picked well. I taught your daddy when he was your age. Perhaps if we get a moment today I can tell you some funny stories about him and your mummy."

A knowing look passed between the two women. A look that spoke of sympathies and strengths, of happy memories and easier times.

Georgie knew her baby was in safe hands. She watched as he walked in, beaming at the prospect of new stories about his daddy. He lived for the tales about Billy, much like she did. As she stood there and watched him go, Georgie could have sworn she felt the lightest touch of lips on her cheek.

"I still miss you," she whispered, placing a hand to her face. "But thank you for giving me the perfect piece of you to remember you by."

ACKNOWLEDGMENTS

Someday was born from a song challenge in the Write Here, Write Now Writer's Community. It started as a short about five hundred words long, then it merged with a piece I'd started hoping to raise awareness on mental health after pregnancy. Of course, what you see here is the finished product and it's a book I'm incredibly proud of.

To get it to this point, however, there are several people I need to thank, so please allow me a moment to gush over their excellence.

As always, I have to thank my other half (some might say better half) for the time he gave me to write, edit, and generally mess around with this document to make it what I wanted it to be. His help and support with my boys, who both put up with Mummy being lost in her words splendidly, is more valuable than he realises.

I've had a great team of readers on this one who went through the early drafts, tweaked it, and helped polish it before edits. I can't thank you enough! I wrote this so long ago that I can't remember who actually had eyes on it. For that reason, I won't list names in case I get them wrong, but please know I appreciate anything you could do to help with my journey on this one.

My editor plays a huge part in my writing journey, and she is an absolute legend. Her feedback on this one made me cry, and I can only hope her feelings about this book are echoed by those who've read it.

Leanne, you're a new one to these shout outs, but gosh

have you earned it. You keep me sane, you talk me down, you build me up—you are amazing and I value your friendship more than I ever thought possible. Combine that with your immense skills for covers, formats, marketing support…don't ever leave me, right?

And, as I always do, I end this with a thanks for you, the person holding this book. Thank you for taking a chance, for trying my words, for loving my characters. Thank you for the reviews, the shares, the likes, for every little thing you do to support me as I try to turn this from a very expensive hobby to something akin to a career. I love you all!

ABOUT THE AUTHOR

T S Arthur is a multi genre author from the UK who enjoys chasing words as they appear to her at random, inconvenient times. A mummy, ex-teacher, and avid reader, she squeezes in writing when the family are napping or busy playing. You'll often find her sat writing whilst being battered by a teddy or plastic axe, or sometimes a cat paw.

Happy to try any genre, her stories mostly feature relatable characters that everyone can enjoy. She has always carried a notebook and held dreams of being an author, although it took longer than planned to get the ball rolling. Whilst her life may be hectic at times, she will always continue building a wide range of stories and characters to help readers achieve that 'escape'.

For more news from T S Arthur, including details on all her books and social media, you can visit her website here: https://tsarthurauthor.co.uk/

OTHER BOOKS BY T S ARTHUR

CONTEMPORARY ROMANCE

Found By Drew

Puddles of Love Book 1

Lost in Lia

Puddles of Love Book 2

SPORTS ROMANCE

Formula Love

An F1 pit lane romance

YA PARANORMAL

Them

A Tempus Series Short Story

Milton Keynes UK
Ingram Content Group UK Ltd.
UKHW011328060724
445042UK00005B/223